Honey for Tea
published by Graffeg March 2016
Copyright © Graffeg Limited 2016
ISBN 9781910862384

Honey for Tea
Text and photographs copyright © Karin Celestine
Designed and produced by Graffeg
www.graffeg.com

Graffeg Limited, 24 Stradey Park Business
Centre, Mwrwg Road, Llangennech, Llanelli,
Carmarthenshire SA14 8YP
Wales UK Tel 01554 824000
www.graffeg.com

1 2 3 4 5 6 7 8 9

For more fun with the Tribe visit
www.celestineandthehare.com

Celestine and the Hare
Honey for Tea
by Karin Celestine

This book belongs to

GRAFFEG

Meet the Tribe

Baby Weasus was found on the doorstep on Christmas Eve and was adopted by King Norty. She is only little but clever and brave and curious with a huge kind heart. Being a weasel she is also a little bit mischievous, especially when with her daddy.

King Norty is the King of the Weasels. He can't read but uses his weaselly intelligence, wit and torrential charm for choklit snaffling. Which is what he spends his days plotting to do (along with being daddy to Baby Weasus).

2

Panda loves the sea and his sock hat. He likes to draw and is best friends with Emily. He is quiet and thoughtful and loves it when Emily reads to him.

Emily is wise and patient and kind and loves to read. She looks after everyone in the Shed and gives the best cuddles. She likes to make things and read books but will always stop what she is doing to hold down the knot on your parcel.

Small doesn't remember what he is or where he came from before he was found but he is small so he is called Small. He is rather quiet and shy and sometimes people don't notice him, but he is very helpful and always kind. He likes to sit in tea cups and eat biscuits and watch what is going on best of all. Everyone loves Small.

Celestine and the Hare

It is a world where weasels are ruled by King Norty, pandas ride space hoppers and bears read stories to each other. It is a place that makes people smile and where kindness is the order of the day. All are welcome.

Karin taught children, about art, about chemistry, numbers, crafts and magic, but she was always drawn back to the Shed where she brings to life creatures of all kinds using only wool, observation and the power of imagination.

Karin and the creatures love stories and kindness, books and choklit and making things, and on Sundays they have Danish pastries but not the apricot ones because they are frankly wrong.

Celestine, her great grandmother and namesake, watches over all in the shed and the hare sits with her; old wisdom helping the Tribe along their path in life.

Karin Celestine lives in a small house in Monmouth, Wales. In her garden there is a shed and in that shed is another world. The world of Celestine and the Hare.

Celestine and the Hare
Honey for Tea

For my dearest Mangi and Klas-Göran
who look after the flowers and bees
so there is always honey for tea.

Emily likes to sit on the plant pot and drink her tea before the rest of the house wakes up. There is something special about the early morning light just as the birds are waking.

She likes a spoon of honey in her tea as she is a bear and bears like honey.

Emily built a beehive in the garden for her friends, the bees, to live in. She grows flowers for the bees and looks after them and they give her honey for her tea.

Emily loves to sit by the hive and watch the bees do their little bee dance. She wears her beekeeper's hat when she sits close to the bees. It is easy to get scared and sting when you are a small bee, even though you don't mean to hurt your friends.

'Can I play with the bees, Emily?' asked Baby Weasus one sunny day when Emily had finished looking after them.

'They are far too busy getting food and making honey to play I'm afraid,' said Emily.

'I like honey,' says Baby Weasus.

'So do I,' said Emily. 'They are our friends the bees. They work very hard to make honey for us.'

'Can I pick some flowers for the bees as a thank you for making us all the honey?' asked Baby Weasus.

'Well, I think they would like it better if you planted some flowers for them,' said Emily.

'Oh yes please can I do that, Emily?'

'But of course you can. What would you like to plant?'

'What do bees like very bestest of all?' asked Baby Weasus.

'Well, my bees like the wild raspberries and the heather that grows by the beach best of all, but they love herbs and sunflowers and wild flowers too. Why don't you get the plant book and choose?'

So Emily got the big plant book down from the shelf and Baby Weasus sat and looked through the book for a long time.

(a) Grey Poplar *Populus canescens* (Ait.) Sm., family Salicaceae. A much planted tree, probably of hybrid origin between the White and Black Poplar. Grows to 30m. Tree with rounded crown. See page 162 and Leaves 164(b).

(h) Aspen *Populus tremula* L., family Salicaceae. A tree native throughout the British Isles. Height to 20m. Common on damp heaths and by water. Flowers March to April. See others this page and Leaves 164(c).

(i) Hybrid Black Poplar *Populus × canadensis*. Hort., family Salicaceae. Freely hybridised. This common tree represents the most hybrids which were crossed between the true Black Poplar *P. nigra* and other species. They are commonly planted trees, put in and on roadsides. See Leaves 164(f) and compare with 164(h).

(k) White Poplar *Populus alba* L., family of the Salicaceae. Tree, introduced. The leaves and shoots leaves are covered with white hairs. Height 30m. See others this page and Leaves 164(g).

(l) Lombardy Poplar *Populus nigra* var *italica* Duroi, family Salicaceae. A much planted tree, introduction. Flowers March. See plates.

(j) Balsam Poplar *Populus gileadensis* Rouleau, family Salicaceae. Tree, to 25m, introduced. Very distinctive smell of balsam from the sticky leaves and buds. Flowers Feb. to March. See others above and Leaves 164(d).

(j) Wych Elm *Ulmus glabra* Huds., family Ulmaceae. A common native tree. Found all over the British Isles though much more common in the north than English Elm 1x(l) and with larger leaves. Flowers Feb. to March. See below and 24(h), 158(b).

(l) English Elm *Ulmus procera* Salisb., family Ulmaceae. A common tree in England and Ireland, rare in Scotland. Height to 30m. Native in hedges and very common. Badly hit by Dutch Elm disease. Flowers Feb. to March. See above 24(f), 158(a).

(m) Hazel or **Cob-nut** *Corylus avellana* L., family Corylaceae. A common native shrub found all over the British Isles. Height to 6m. A magical plant, divining rods are made from it. Hazel was grown in oak woods and coppiced, the wood used for hurdles and wattle and daub buildings. Flowers Jan. to March. See Leaves 164(e).

(n) Alder *Alnus glutinosa* (L.) Gaertn., family Betulaceae. A very common native tree found all over the British Isles. To a height of 20m. Grows in wet places. Flowers Feb. to March. See Leaves 158(c).

(o) Pussy Willow, Goat Willow or **Great Sallow** *Salix caprea* L., family Salicaceae. A very common shrub found all over the British Isles; less common in Ireland. Height to 10m. Flowers March to April. The rest of the willows have leaves only illustrated. See 166(c)–(m).

'I think I should like to plant some chives,' she said. 'It says bees love them and you can eat them as well. I can grow some on my windowsill too in case a lost bee gets stuck and is hungry in the night when I can't let it out because I am sleeping.'

'That's a very good choice,' said Emily. 'I have some chive seeds in my seed tin.'

Emily found a plant pot and put it down near the alder tree. Baby Weasus spent the afternoon planting the chive seeds. She poked a little hole in the soil, dropped a seed in, and then covered it over and patted it gently. She then watered it with her jug as she wasn't big enough to pick up the watering can. All the time she watched the bees buzzing around looking for blossoms and wishing they would stop to play with her.

The alder tree had given Emily an idea. While Baby Weasus was busy with her seeds, Emily climbed the alder tree to look for the tiny cones that grow on them. Bears are good at climbing trees.

She collected a bundle of the brown
ripe cones and took them back to
the house.

Emily found some yellow wool and tissue paper. When Baby Weasus came in for tea, she showed her how she could use the cones to make some bees to play with. Emily helped Baby Weasus with the scissors because she is still rather small and can't reach both sides yet.

Emily hung the bees up above Baby Weasus and then they made toast and honey for tea.

'Thank you, Emily. I love my bees. When my chives grow can I take my bees to see them?'

'Yes of course you can, Baby Weasus. They might even meet a real bee who is happy that you planted the flowers.'

'I hope so,' said Baby Weasus and took a huge bite of her toast...

How to make alder cone bees

Find an alder tree... they like to grow near
water so look by river banks or by a pond
in the park. They are also planted on city
streets sometimes so keep a look out.
The cones fall down in the autumn so
you can pick them up.

You need some yellow wool.
Knitters will often give you a
piece of wool if you ask them.
You don't need much. Just the
length of this book for a bee.

32

Wrap the wool around the
cone in a spiral and push it
between the gaps in the cone.

33

Take a piece of tissue paper and fold it in half. Draw half a wing shape on the paper and cut it out, leaving the fold uncut. To get the wings the right size for your bee, draw around the cone on the fold.

Open out and poke the
middle of the wings into
the cone.

Use the end of a pencil or your fingers to poke it in.

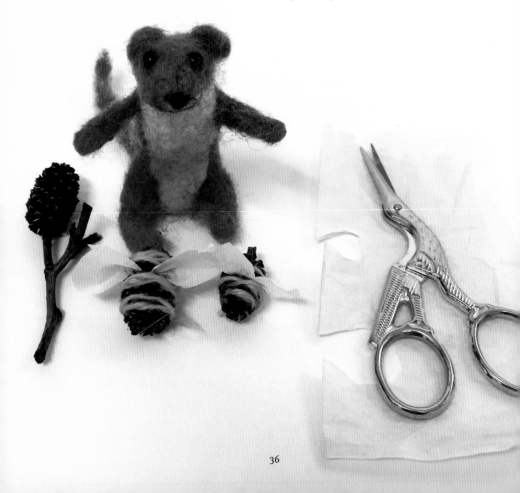

Take some sewing thread and wrap it around the cone a few times over the middle of the wings to hold them in place and leave it sticking up from the middle.

Cut it long enough to hang the bee
up. You can make lots of bees and
tie them onto a stick. It looks best if
you put them at different heights.

How to plant flowers for bees

Gardeners will often give you a few seeds if
you ask them or you can buy packets of seeds
specially chosen because the bees like them.
Flowers are good food for other insects too like
butterflies, so you will be helping lots of wildlife.
Hedgehogs like to eat slugs that come to eat the
plants so if you are really lucky you might see a
hedgehog one day too.

Dig a little hole in the earth and drop your seed in. Once you have dropped the seed in, tuck it in with some earth on top and give it a little water.

You can use a marker to show where your seeds are planted. You could use a lollipop stick or make one from cut up pieces of plastic like a yoghurt pot. Or you can just scatter seeds everywhere and wait for a lovely surprise.

Keep watering your seed as it grows and pull up any weeds that get in the way.

Sometimes weeds are just as lovely as the plant you are trying to grow, they are just in the wrong place, so you could dig them up and replant them elsewhere in the garden.

Seed packets always tell you what to do on the back of them, but if you are not sure ask someone in your Tribe who likes to garden. They are always happy to help a young gardener.

If you don't have a garden, a pot or a window box is lovely. Or you could ask at school if you can plant something there.

Bees need flowers for food. They help us and are important. Ask at the library or your school for help to find out more about bees and how to grow flowers for them. You could even find out how to become a beekeeper like Emily.